Sing A Song of Murder

Allen Barker hit the big time. All of a sudden everything he did turned to gold or platinum. He had found his dream. He was a superstar.

Then his girlfriends started getting murdered. One, those things happen. Two, a sad thing. Was he jinxed? Would there be a third? That would be a long way over mere coincidence.

Who would be doing this? Why?

Contents

The Big Break pg. 1
Investigation Begins pg. 14
On the Road Again pg. 25
A Little Subterfuge pg. 39
Plans pg. 50
Dark Corners pg. 58

About the author

CD Moulton has traveled extensively over much of the world both in the music business, where he was a rock guitarist, songwriter and arranger and in an import/export business. He has been everything from a bar owner to auto salvage (junkyard) manager, longshoreman to high steel worker, orchid grower to landscaper, tropical fish farmer to commercial fisherman. He started writing books in 1983 and has published more than 350 books as of January 1, 2023. His most popular books to date are about research with orchids, though much of his science fiction and fantasy work has proven popular. He wrote the CD Grimes, PI series, and the Det. Nick Storie series, Clint Faraday series, and many other works.

He now resides in Gualaca, Chiriqui, Panamá, where he writes books, plays music with friends, does research with orchids and medicinal plants. He has lately become involved in fighting for the rights of the indigenous people, who are among his closest friends, and in fighting the extreme corruption in the courts and police in Panamá.

He offers the free e-book, *Fading Paradise*, that explains what he has been through because of the corruption.

CD is the discoverer of the Chadam Protocol for curing cancer.

Facebook page Ambrosia peruviana for cancer.

<u>The Big Break</u>

Allen Barker, real name, Allen Barker, walked out on the stage. He tipped his white Stetson, slung the guitar across his shoulder, and said, "This is one I wrote about a girl who is very, very special to me. I've tried to say what I feel. That's what music is about to me. That's my communication.

"Guys, 'A' with a 'D' break."

He played an intricate intro, moved to the mike, and sang:

I was waiting for the bus when you walked by
I was trying to decide the way to try
It wasn't worth the effort
If you know what ...

"Bullshit! That's crap! Sorry I even thought of doing anything like that.

"This is the way it is. I sing what I really feel and say what I really want to say or I leave this place tonight and never look back. I'm a damned good mechanic. That works for me with cars and trucks. I don't want to be a mechanic with my music. There are thousands of those playing the bar scene.

"Yeah. It pays the bills – but so what? You're a cheap whore!

"I'm not a whore! No more!

"So. Where do I go from here? I can sing a hundred songs you all know and like and be another grain of sand ...

"I have an idea. If you guys can figure out what I'm trying to do, join in. It's not going to be quite the standard kind of thing. It floats or it sinks.

"I'll try it in 'C.' Here goes."

You're not another grain of sand on an endless beach.

You're not another sexy little peach.

You're not a girl who's ripe for picking, not another bimbo pixie,

You're special.

Lou Ann, I saw you waiting for a train.

I knew right then I'd want to know your name.

You saw me and the sparks began to fly.

You weren't another so-so passer-by.

You're different-

I don't know how to say just what I feel.

I can't express in words sufficient-

The depth and meaning of your appeal.

You lit a fire that's deep within me.

You made me see what in my lonely life is real...

"Damn! More crap! I have to break out of this stupidity!

"Remember CCR? John Fogerty?

"I like to play around with things in styles that impress me. This is one I was fooling around with the other day. We were, to be honest about it, a little drunk. I always thought Fogerty was one of the best. He invented a music style.

"It's not country, but it's not not country. It's sort of crossover."

He hit a hard 'D':

Come on, to the party,
Jump in, the water's fine.
Can't wait, to get started,
Ain't no better time.
You can move along with the feeling.
You can stay all night.
Grab the old lady and come on over.
Make you feel so right.
When you reach the party,
Bring a song to sing...

He went on for four verses, making up the last two as he went. The audience was really getting into it. He was lightheaded. He didn't seem to know what to say next. It just came out. Nothing like this had ever happened before. He finally knew what it meant to connect with an audience. He understood what was meant when the older musicians described a night and said, "What a rush!"

He had a few songs in his head that he'd written that he didn't think would make it. They were fringe country/rock.

Well, country was now like the older rock, where there was music and melody and sense to the words.

He did a few numbers that were like Fleetwood Mac or Bob Seger, with a heavier rock influence.

Face it! They had hits that were accepted by country, rock, pop, and what have you. Music said things. The Eagles were everywhere, even in some countries that didn't speak English. *Hotel California* was one of the most-played numbers worldwide.

Me and Bobby McGhee, After the Glitter Fades – even Moody Blues did things that were just plain country. They were accepted by all types of music.

He didn't remember a lot about the night. He knew he "Hit the vein" with some things.

He stayed on the stage longer than ever before. He didn't realize the place was supposed to close at two, but he played until after three thirty. They closed the doors and let the people decide when to close. The sheriff was supposed to make everyone leave by two thirty, but two cops were there and part of the audience.

He found out later, the next morning when he

got a call, that an agent for a big recording company was there and wanted to talk with him.

He'd heard that before. Some independent agent who knew someone at a studio who knew someone who did scouting whose sister's boyfriend had an in with.

He did have a good voice. He did have the ability to sing the smooth love songs or the teary blues or the growl of real rock.

What the hell. He said he'd talk with the turkey. All it would cost was a little time.

He felt really good. The rush from last night had his energy levels way up.

He cleaned up and went down to the restaurant, where two suits were sitting. He introduced himself. They were Arnold Farthing and George Fledger. They said to have a seat, order anything he wanted . They wanted him in a good mood. They wanted to sign him with their company. It would make them and him. They had big money backing them.

"Al, we own the company. I'll be honest and tell you that we are owned. It's sort of mob, but legitimate. Some of the older style mobsters have found that going legit makes a lot of sense and a lot of money. They know how the business works and know promotion can make even something as sick and empty as rap pay off," Fledger said. "We were looking for something to get started. We thought we could find someone with a little appeal to a cult group and build on it. We were told about your voice and your charm – what was called charisma a few years ago – and came to see if we could work you into something.

"When you started, we both rolled our eyes and decided the one drink, then split. Another bomb.

"We liked your voice. We didn't like what you were doing with it.

"You seemed sincere when you said you were spouting crap, then you went into fusion and ... we stayed until the two cops said the show was over, that everyone was tired. Go home.

"You're it.

"We can take you and let you run where you want to go. We don't have to spend the ten million building up a promo kit. You did that last night. Take a flier with us and we can all go to the top."

"Before you say to kiss your ass, let me say we can offer a contract no one can top. It's spec," Farthing said. "We'll make it a contract you can void or we can void, with reason.

"That will protect us both. If last night was a once in a lifetime thing, we have a way out. If you find we're not giving you an honest break, you can opt out.

"You sounded like a hippie last night. Minus the drugs. The philosophy.

"Drugs are one thing we won't put up with, and that's in the contract. I've had 'way too much experience with that."

Al looked from one to the other. He wanted to trust them, but he knew what agents were.

"I use pot, but not much. I write the things like last night when I'm using. I don't and won't use anything stronger."

"I have a little bit of an issue with it. Arny doesn't," Fledger said. "We can make some kind of arrangement ... I don't know."

"Pot's legal in a couple of states now," Al pointed out. "I can be a total asshole with booze. I control how much I drink very carefully. I'm mellow with pot. I like a little red wine and a toke or two, then music.

"I don't use it more than maybe once a month. I never smoke a whole joint. As I said, a toke or two.

"I might be interested. I like to take the big chance. You can win big or lose big. Adrenalin rush, I guess."

"How about we put in the contract that use of any milder drug is permitted so long as it doesn't affect your speech or actions in a negative way?" Arny suggested. George agreed that would be acceptable.

"Well, we're talking about the wording of a contract. May I assume you're willing to take a chance?" Arny asked.

"I suppose. I can always go back to my day job. I'm one hell of a good mechanic."

"We'll work out a contract. You can be there with suggestions," George said. They agreed.

Al figured he had nothing to lose until he signed the thing. If he was sure they meant it when they said it would be breakable for cause, he would take a chance.

They worked out a contract. One page. Clear and simple. No technicalities with the wording.

He signed. George handed him a check for ten thousand dollars.

"I know it's nowhere near what most get, but we're just starting. With your contract you're as much as a partner.

"Make us a million, buddy, and you make yourself a million."

They hadn't discussed a signing fee. They said they could spend quite a bit, but had to keep it to where a sort of, face it, laundering scheme wouldn't be exposed.

He was to make a video of *The Party* as soon as they could work out the script.

"How about, I walk out on the stage and do it?

There are some people dancing right there. A keg. People letting loose and enjoying themselves. Maybe a pretty girl flirting with me as I sing it.

"Pretty. Not a sex-bomb ass-shaking bimbo. That's not me. Simple, cheap, effective."

They jumped on that!

Allen Barker walked out on the stage, grinned at the audience, and sat on a stool.

The bass started a heartbeat with the drums. Wilma, a pretty girl with blue eyes and reddish-blond hair, wearing what was almost a fifties red bop dress and sneakers walked across the stage, stopped, cocked her head to the side, smiled, and went on with a speculative look.

Whoa-oh!
Here she comes,
Dressed in red.
Shake that thing, baby,
Twist my head.
The lady's got it,
She has no doubts.
You can spot it,
When she walks out.
Whoa-oh!
Take me to another plane,
Wake me up to pleasant pain,
Love me Momma,

Whoa-oh!
A wild screaming guitar break.
Whoa-oh!
There she goes.
Leaves a tingle,
Head to toe.
She has got it,
I have no doubt.
I could spot it,
When she walked out.
Love me again, Momma!
Whoa-oh!
The insistent beat and the look of fun he projected brought the house down. Annette Gooden, the girl he was going with, even getting serious about, strutted across the stage, turned to give him a come-on look over her shoulder, and off the other side of the stage. That was as big as his leering grin.

He didn't let the mood fade.
Help me!
I'm falling in lust.
Free me, Baby,
Make me trust,
What you say, Honey,
Makes me hog wild.
Don't need money,
With this love child.

It was as big as before. He was good at arrangement. He had the breaks and the full rock sound, but with a country flavor that couldn't be denied. Folk had steel guitars. Rock very seldom did. He was a hit with both genre.

He was climbing the charts with his first CD. He had sold-out concerts before the heavy promo started. He had the world by the tail, as the saying went. The pre-orders for the CD would make him and his agent/partners millionaires. He had the voice, but didn't depend on that. He also had the talent to do the arrangement and video bit. His videos were very effective, but very simple. No waving the arms and sexy semi-nude bimbos shaking and hanging all over an ugly no-talent jerk. Wilma and Annette strutting across the stage with the come-on look would be featured on the video. Toward the end they would be to the side, giggling and trading secrets. They were the high point.

That was his philosophy. Simple and honest. If it's about love, make it about deep feelings. If it's about a romp, make it fun and shallow. Make what the music said say what the song said. Make the videos follow the song, not the other way around. Don't have things in the videos that have nothing to do with the lyrics. Don't get vulgar for the sake of being vulgar. Shock value went out in the seventies. Helll-oo-oo!

He spent awhile in the afternoon rehearsing with the band. They didn't really need it. He had a habit of writing a song onstage. He was loyal to the guys, they were loyal to him. They got a better than average cut of the proceeds. He had a great dinner with Annette, then went to help set up the stage. Every show had at least one new number. He and a couple of people in the band could write songs on any subject. Filler stuff, mostly, but they more often than with most people, tended to appeal, to make the charts. The art was in presenting them.

The show had four very pretty girls. They were dressed normally and walked and danced normally. Al had noticed at one show awhile back that featured a popular group with the half-naked shaking bimbos that his girls with their demure manners and revealing but not porno-sexy dress ended up more popular than the bimbos. His girls didn't do the bumps and grinds. They swayed with the music or danced an exotic dance that was erotic as all hell, but not even close to pornographic. No big ass and big tits. Lithe shapely bodies. Annette didn't dance or appear, though the audiences wanted her. She did choreography and was at the shows.

She wasn't there that night. Al didn't know why.

Paul, the bass man, said she was there earlier, but left when she got a phone call.

Al didn't think too much about it until he was in the hotel. She didn't come in and didn't leave a message or call him.

At four fifteen in the morning he got the message that her body was found at the picnic site near the river. She had been strangled.

Det. Cliff Howard looked at the new superstar sitting across the desk. He was a good judge of people. This man was deeply hurt and grieving. He was appearing on a stage in front of fifty thousand people when Annette was murdered. Allen Barker (vocals, rhythm guitar), Paul Russo (bass), Sam Carlson (lead guitar), Andy Wright (keyboards) Billy Hardin (give him an instrument, he could play it), Jim Baker (lights) and Lyle Granger (sound) were out as the killer. They were on that stage. Wilma progress, Sarah Flanders, John Bender, Gladys Manners and Alice Dawn were on the stage at times, so wouldn't have the time to go out to where the murder took place.

Cliff liked to start a case by eliminating suspects. It gave him the people he could believe. This was the first time the Allen Barker Connection had played in Florida south of Jacksonville. Tampa was a big market. Cliff couldn't believe anyone not with the show could be the killer. He would go with that theory unless and until someone else was brought into it.

Annette was from Ashville, Kentucky. She had

never been in the area before. She had no relatives or friends here. She would not go anywhere with a stranger. She did the flirty part onstage in the past. Allen did the randy songs, but they were strictly straight-arrow with each other. He was going to marry her in three months. She had not been sexually assaulted at the murder scene. She tended to be a private person. She made friends easily.

She didn't use makeup, except for light lipstick. She was a natural beauty. She didn't need it. She was the type a lot of men would shy away from. She was the type you got serious with, fast. A lot of men didn't want that.

Cliff was just getting started with the investigation. A quick rundown on everyone with the show didn't give him a hint of a likely. The show was backed by semi-mobster types. None of the backers were anywhere near Tampa. Nashville was the closest connection, but the real backers were from California and Texas. Only two others were with the show. They were sitting out front with the members of the band. Arny Farthing and George Fledger. They were agents and partners with Barker. Very unusual. Everyone got along with them.

Al had no answers. He had thousands of questions. Most were the same questions Cliff had. The two seemed to click. Al wanted this solved. He wanted ten hours alone with whoever killed Annette. He would make it take that long to die. The bastard son of a bitch would spend nine hours and fifty nine minutes begging Al to let him die.

Six hours of questions and testimony. Cliff interviewed every one of them. He had to find some connection, someone who had a motive, no matter how weak, to kill Annette. There didn't seem to be any. The show was like a big family. They would snap at each other about some little thing now and then, but nothing serious.

The show tonight was cancelled. The fifty four thousand sold tickets would be refunded or could be held until the show went on. The band agreed they had an obligation, not to the money people and promoters or backers, to the audience.

They weren't booked anywhere next week. They would do the show next Saturday instead of today.

"I don't think I can go out there ... Maybe I can. I won't be good," Al said dejectedly. "We owe them a show.

"Goddamn it! 'The show must go on' was a great line! I never thought I'd have to live it!"

Allen Barker walked out onto the stage. The

audience was silent. He had thought of hundreds of songs to start this show, but simply couldn't think of anything. He might do the Elton John number, *Candle in the Wind*, but that wasn't all he wanted to say. It had been awhile since he did anyone else's songs.

He sat on the stool.

"Good evening. I'll try to ... do something that's not too down.

"I might ... I remember a line. Maybe it will fit."

He picked the guitar off the stand and did a little run. Bluesy. Not quite right. Don't start the show on a downer. They don't need that. They didn't pay for that.

Sometimes we have to live ways that we don't choose.

Sometimes we all must sing the heartbreak blues.

Time will change things, no matter how we fight.
Time can often make heavy things more light.
Life gives us pleasure, life gives us pain,
Life gives us help, life gives us strain.
Throughout it all we try to make it past
Those things that sometimes stop us in our paths.
We hide our pain, we hide our grief.
We have to live inside beliefs.
After all, the show must go on.

He did an intricate run, bouncing off the blues box, adding hammers and slides.

The show must go on and on and on.
She said that to me many times, you see.
We owe each other many things at times.
What seems impossible to bear
Will be put to the other side somewhere
Until we come to terms with what life gives.
We have to try to be more positive.
As much as we sometimes wish it won't
We start and stop and then we do or don't
Continue with a sad and hopeless line.
After all, the show must go on.

He did a fast breaking run and stop. The audience was silent for a moment, then a few clapped. It was soon so loud it hurt his ears. The audience was standing and ... not cheering. Offering him their help, somehow.

He fought back the tears. He said, very quietly, "Thank you. You can't know how much I need you right now."

Then he gave them the show of a lifetime. He wrote most of it right then and there. The band couldn't follow him well in parts. It was things they'd never done before. Paul got so screwed up in a bass pattern he said, "Shit! Damn it to hell!" a little too close to a mike. The audience laughed. The mood was lighter. The band members made jokes of the mistakes. Andy threw up his hands when he messed up a solo. Everyone laughed so hard they had to stop until they could get back into sync. Jim put the wrong spots on the wrong person a couple of times. The audience picked up the simple chorus lines in a couple and sang along. It was sad, but hopeful, then more hopeful, then light. That audience took away a lot of the pain.

Billy came close near the end while sharing a contrast lead with Al. No mikes. He said, "Annette would want it this way. You know that." Al nodded. It was true.

The show went over more than an hour. Al was exhausted when he hit the bed, not even taking off his shoes.

He cried himself to sleep. Not in grief, but because of what that audience and his band said and gave to him.

Cliff was offstage and out of sight for part of the show and in the audience for part. He tried to stay out of the sight of the performers. He knew they couldn't see much because of the lights. He came across Arny and George near the main entrance. George said, "What a hell of a sick way to make music history!"

They attended part of the shows. This was a new

venue, so they were here. They would move among the audience to hear what people were saying, to get reactions. Tonight, they had mostly observed.

"Well, another platinum CD before it's recorded. We have six different spots we record a show, video and audio. Studio quality. This will be a live performance extended CD. We have the angles and sound," Arny said. "Sorry. I can't help it. I think of the business angles only during a show. It's my nature."

"We can both look insensitive as hell," George agreed. "We got greedy fast when Al hit it so big. We never had more than a couple thou, got minimum backing, and are overnight millionaires.

"We do feel very sad for Al, for Annette. It's a terrible thing."

They chatted for a few minutes, then Cliff circulated more. He saw how the audience took a bit of the pain from Al. He didn't know how that happened, but it did. Al had the true love of these people. His songs and his manner made him a part of them, not someone somewhere else who appealed to them in small ways. Cliff envied him that.

When the show broke up he went back to the station, made a report, and went home, himself.

In the morning Al went to the studio they had

rented to help edit the videos for the CD. It wasn't something he wanted to do, but he had to keep busy or go crazy. At first, he wanted to leave out some of the gaffs, but soon saw they made the show something that the audience was participating in. It gave the concert the flavor of impromptu performance. It was him reacting to the audience and the audience reacting to him.

He managed to get engrossed in it, selecting the best angle, superimposing angles at a couple of points to make a very effective statement. This really was a tribute to Annette. It was the entire audience sharing their love and grief.

The guys came in. Billy got a kick out of when he threw his hands in the air, Paul said his comment, as jumbled as it was, made it real for him. Andy said he first thought it would make him seem like a fool, then realized it added to the lightening of the mood.

Annette's name was mentioned just one time, right at the first. Somehow, the whole show had her front and center.

"Well," George said, when they had it as good as it was going to be. "What do we call it? Anybody got a suggestion?"

"Godspeed, Annette," Pal suggested. "I see a cover picture on the CD. The spot where ... where Billy blew the solo. A superimposition of

Annette's face. Smiling. Like she would have if she saw that.

"She was there. At the show. We all felt it."

"I like it. I really like it," Al said. "I have the picture. I call it her impish grin, not a smile. It was from that time I got the words crossed in *Walk In Love*. In Austin. You remember that. The camera caught it perfectly. I have several prints of it."

"Perfect!" Arny cried. "The show was a tribute that will be a classic forever. Every damned song was performed for the first time right there. What a great tribute!"

They worked for a time getting just the right image, then superimposing the semi-transparent face.

It was after midnight when they all went to their hotel, but it was a productive day. The program was sent to the manufacturer in California. There would be a hundred thousand copies of the CD on the stands by noon Monday and another hundred thousand the following day.

"Fifty thousand will come on the first flight tonight," Arny promised. "Everyone at that concert will want a copy.

"Let's not cheapen this. Only those who were at the show can get a signature on the CD. Show a stub and get the signed CD. No stub, no signing.

"You arms are going to be so tired you can't move them before the day's done. You've had big signings before, but this will be huge."

The shipment came. There were several huge crates of the CDs. It was just seven thirty and there was a line of people all the way around the block. Arny had posters printed telling about the CD and the terms of sale of signed copies. They were hanging on anywhere they found the space. Al said what about the ones who threw the stubs away at the concert. Paul answered that no one who was at that concert was about to throw away the stub.

Arny and George would check the stubs before they would sell the CD, which the guys had spent two hours before the opening signing. They would continue until all were gone. When they took a break to ease the cramp in their hands they went out front to chat with their fans. A TV crew showed up and it became a festive occasion. No one seemed to mind standing in line for two hours or more.

50,000 CDs were delivered, 50,000 sold by five fifteen PM. Arny had more than three hundred thousand dollars, in cash. Five thousand more would arrive tonight and be sold tomorrow. There were 54,000 people at the concert.

They were all totally exhausted.

Cliff had come to the sale/signing. The guys gave him a CD with all their signatures.

Just before they went for a meal, him invited, Arny announced that there were orders for more than two million copies of the CD over the nation. The signing had gone national on TV, along with an explanation. The manufacturer would produce the two million copies by pausing the production of several others. After all, these were sold before they were recorded!

They soon went to eat a late meal and sack out.

Cliff went to the station. He was getting a small glimmering of an idea.

He had a covert warrant delivered to the bank. It was for the account where all monies from the sales went. The least it would do is show how many million dollars were deposited to that account more than CDs manufactured could account for. That would be a motive. It would also mean the murder could very well be a hit, the person sponsoring the hit in some palatial mansion in California or Texas.

The band would move on day after tomorrow for a concert in Chicago. Cliff would not close the investigation because of that.

On the Road Again

Al had done two concerts since the Tampa one. He was, at last, getting to where he wasn't so down so much. That was a phase where he wrote a lot of songs, many of them not to his own liking, though the public seemed to like them. He would have to do them, a few at the time, in other concerts. They had so many hits it was necessary to make at least half the show older numbers. They did change small parts, lead guitar, inflection, pacing. Some were improved over the original.

They did one concert a month, now.

Al met Donna Andrews. She caught his attention the first time he saw her. She was a natural beauty, but was very different from Annette in many ways. She was more serious.

They took only a month to decide they fit together very well. She saw that Al's randy songs were for fun and entertainment. He wasn't at all like that. The concerts lightened up considerably. It was back to more like when they started.. They were still bestsellers, but it had dropped to a more reasonable level. Al said the market was stabilized for their work. The stock market could go up and down, they would always have a following who would be depended upon.

They all had more than they knew what to do with. They could do the shows because of their love of music.

After the second month with Donna Al announced they would be married in two months, after the end of the year tour. They would be married on the first of January, starting a new life with the new year.

The next concert was in Atlanta, Georgia, then the end of the year in New York.

Hey, Babe, you really caught my eye.
I saw you by the river side.
You fit your clothes so very well.
Your smile had a story, I could tell.
Your walk could make a strong man cry.
I knew right then that I would try
To have you,
To hold you,
To love you,
To ... oh ... to know you.
A minute when a man is weak
Can lead to hell or to a peak
Of love or hate or something new
To having something you should do

To get from under
Life's major blunder
Can put asunder
What I ... oh ... now know
So turn away and wag your tail.
You'll soon attract another male.
To fall into your evil trap.
To wander far from any map.
To heaven.
Or hell.
Or whatever.
To ... oh ... to here.
Bartender, more beer!

The crowd loved it. He didn't much like it. It was empty and silly, but was okay for concerts like this. It was by request. He did a few at the end of the concerts.

Billy exclaimed, "No! God! No!" just loud enough for him to hear. Some man from backstage had come to tell him something. Al raised an eyebrow at Billy, who came to whisper, "It's Donna. Close the concert. We're overtime, anyhow."

Al leaned to the mike. "A minute, please."

He turned back to Billy. "What? Is she in trouble? Is she alright?"

Billy looked very much in pain. "She's ... dead."

Al was frozen in shock for a few seconds. He

suddenly screamed, "No! Not again! No! This is a sick joke!"

Billy looked helpless. Paul and Andy came running up to him. He slung the guitar off his shoulder and slammed it on the stage. He stood for a few seconds, then stalked off.

"Bad news," Billy announced on the mike. "Concert's over. There's been a tragedy."

They went backstage. Al was being held by two cops. One kept saying to calm down. It wouldn't solve anything for him to go running wild.

George and Arny came running in, demanding to know what was the matter. Billy told them. He said they knew about his former girlfriend being murdered. It had happened again.

"Killed? I mean ... killed? How? Who?" Arny asked.

"Same as Annette. Strangled."

"Donna?" George asked, puzzled. "Who would want to hurt Donna? She doesn't know anyone here."

He turned to a policeman who was trying to calm Al down. "Call Tampa, Florida. A policeman named Cliff Something handled the case where Al's other girlfriend was murdered. He may have information you can use.

"This is terrible! It can't be happening! It just can't!"

"I'm Frank Greco. I'll be heading this investigation," a bullish man announced. "You say there was another murder? Like this one?

"I'll call Florida, but I need information now.

"The time of death was about an hour and a half ago. I'll have to know where everyone was and what they were doing and who can back them up. I need to know who the dead person knew here. You're all under suspicion, so don't get all huffy about it. That act won't get you anywhere here!"

The whole crew took an instant dislike toward him. That wasn't a smart way to get help from anyone. Al could see that the other policemen there didn't much care for Frank Greco.

"If I might point out a little something, it could save you some time," Arny said, acidly.

"Yeah? What?"

"We were doing a show in front of forty eight thousand six hundred thirty people for the past three hours. Exactly what kind of suspicion could we be under?"

"Uh! Er, we would take that into consideration, of course."

"I imagine you would."

That deflated Greco. His big bad tough cop act was shot to hell. He'd made himself look like an idiot.

"Transferred here from Detroit two weeks ago

when Cpt. Forbes retired. Forbes was damned good. This one, we don't really think will make it. Thinks we're all ignorant savages, y'all," the cop holding Al said.

"You can let me go. I'm in control. You can thank that asshole for that!" Al said. "We played Detroit a year ago. It wasn't so bad, but we weren't exposed to homicide cops there. Tampa, Cliff was a friend. He tried everything he could, but there weren't any clues. Period. It was a lot like here. No one knew anyone from there.

"It does seem strange that the same way was used on the two. It would have to be someone from the show. One of my socalled best friends, but we were all right out there. It doesn't make sense!"

"Were the same people with the show there? Anyone new we can eliminate?

"I promise you that I'll go after this one if Greco doesn't. I'll call Florida and try to find the cop there."

Al took out a card case and looked at the address book inside.

"Cliff Howard, Detective Lieutenant, Homicide and violent crimes, Tampa, Florida. Home phone is here. You can write it down."

"Let me try something." He called to Greco that he was taking Al into the office to get a statement.

He was onstage the entire time, so was definitely not a suspect. Greco waved a hand. He was stalking around, trying to look busy. The cop waved and he and Al went into the little stage manager's office there.

"I'm Ken Goodson. I'll use this phone, if you okay it."

Al nodded. He didn't have the authority to tell anyone they could use the phone or anything else there. "It's one o'clock in the morning there. He'll be home and royally pissed to get a call."

Ken grinned and called the home phone. It was answered after nine rings by Cliff's wife. She gave him the phone. Ken told him who it was and why he was calling.

Ken and Cliff got into a deep discussion. Ken took notes. The call lasted for half an hour. Greco finally came in to say they were wrapping up here. They would go over all the information he had in the morning and see exactly who wasn't telling quite all the truth.

"We were, as you've noted, out there in front of a few thousand people. What could be not quite the truth about that?" Al asked, innocently.

"Oh, someone could pull a disappearing act and no one would know," Greco answered.

"Like who? If anyone left the stage, those thousands would know it."

"Not if it was the sound man or the light man or those."

"They wouldn't notice when someone moved to a dead mike or said something in front of a live mike that wasn't part of the show? Really? If the spot didn't follow the person on lead or vocals? Really?"

"I don't like your attitude!"

"Ask me if I give a shit. I'll answer that I don't give a shit."

"Sir. This man certainly couldn't leave the stage. He was the one featured almost exclusively."

"Grunt!" Greco walked out. Ken said into the phone, "The one I told you about. In charge. Whoopee shit!"

They talked another few minutes, then Ken and Al went back to the backstage area with the others. No one was impressed with Greco – in a way he might have wanted to impress them.

There was nothing they could do. They went to the hotel. Before they left, Al asked Ken, "Cliff have anything that might help?"

"A personal suspicion that it was ordered from somewhere else. The huge money from your tribute album let someone launder about eighty million."

"I see. I never thought of that. I knew some mobsters were backers, but ... if they did anything like that I'll see every one of them hang out to dry. I can get some information, I think. I'll listen a bit more carefully when people talk."

"Be careful. Money is the world and life and all that to those cruds. Get in their way, they eliminate the problem the only way they know."

"But then I wouldn't be there to make them all that money. The laundering would have to stop until they had something else, and it wouldn't be as big."

Ken grinned a dry grin. "Could be!"

They went to the hotel. Al considered what Ken said. He was holding himself under control with a lot of effort. If he found something, he would personally repay the slimy asshole bastard son of a bitch, with huge interest.

He had to take a Xanax for the first time in his life. He did get some sleep, but he didn't get any rest.

In the morning he went to the restaurant. He wasn't hungry, but knew he had to keep his strength up, and not just physical strength. Ken came in about ten. He said he was taking two shifts today. He had convinced Greco he had become a buddy to the big star. He could be around if someone said the wrong thing.

"He wants me to see what kind of drugs you're using and how much. You musicians are all on something. He knew that much. All those songs about marijuana and coke and that proved that! Mark his words! Drugs are behind it!"

"We're famous for being dead-set against drugs, other than *legal* pot."

"All an act! All to keep suspicion off of you! Mark his words!"

"So. What did you say?"

"That I damned well did mark his words. I didn't say to throw them back into his teeth for him."

Al said, "Even that would go a mile over his head. He's an idiot. Political?"

"We so suspect."

Ken sat with all of them. He said to relax and think of something else. Write some music. Something might pop into your mind when you least expect it.

"How many times have you suddenly said, 'Damn! I knew that all along! Why didn't I think of it?' It happens to all of us."

They agreed.

George came in to ask if they would be in any shape to stage the end of the year concert. Arny said they had a contract. They had to do it. "We've made promises. We have to keep them. We can cancel the next couple, but this one, well, we can't get around. It's got to be done."

George shook his head. Ken looked at Arny like

he didn't believe it.

"True, George?" Al asked.

George went to his briefcase to take out a contract. He studied it.

"Damn! It's there! We can't get out of it and stay in business! They'll clean us out

"Why in hell did we sign a contract like this! I'm so sure I know what they say I skip over clause one hundred fifty! Shit!"

"I was going to cancel, but that Anderson guy said we couldn't. I read it. I didn't believe it, either," Arny said.

Al held his hand out for the contract. It was there.

"Well, we have to do it. I intend to keep this contract exactly."

"What do you mean?" Arny asked.

"It doesn't say which numbers we have to perform, does it? We don't have to add one single new song to it. We don't have to perform even one gold or platinum.

"They still have to guarantee us a minimum of one point five million."

"But! ... What will that do to the band's reputation?!" Arny cried.

"I don't give a happy shit!" The others agreed. Ken shook his head.

"Why would they put something like that in a

contract?" Ken asked. They looked around at each other.

"Because of the tribute CD," Arny said.

"Then they'd have to know the murder would happen, wouldn't they?" Ken asked. Shocked looks went around. Ken was about to say something else, but thought better of it. Al nodded the least bit.

The concert was over. The Allen Barker Connection did a review of the things from the preceding year. Most there knew a lot of them. They did have a good time and did find it worth the price. This was a concert that would make a lot of money, but nothing like most of them. It was announced before the gig that it would be a review. No one expected new material.

After the concert, which went exactly to the time the contract demanded, the band met in the hotel. They would skip January and do the next gig in February. The January contract was breakable. There wouldn't be a new CD until then.

They went to their individual homes until the week before the Miami concert. They would see what kind of mood they could carry there.

Al called Cliff two weeks before the concert. He said he had a new girlfriend of sorts. He would introduce her. He's pay if Cliff and wife wanted

to come to the concert. They would be quests of
the band and would stay in the same hotel.

While he was at it, he called Ken. He said Ken
and wife or girlfriend were to be guests of the
band for the Miami gig. Ken had stayed in contact
with Cliff. They hadn't let this case go. They
would never let it go. Greco had dead-filed it.

Al had written new songs. He couldn't com-
pletely break his mood about Donna and Annette.

He was ready to quit this end of the music. He
would do independent walk-ons with new
material. He had more than seventy million
dollars in the bank. He had invested in things that
made a lot. He was always lucky in that kind of
thing.

The band understood. They had it made, themselves. They stayed together because it was that
band with those people. They might get together
once a year for a concert somewhere that would
make an obscene amount of money. Al liked that
idea. He could write the good ones and toss the
ninety percent crap. He said it was to be kept in
the band. He didn't want agents and promoters
and the backers to have time to do anything to
stop him.

This concert, he had a couple that would be as
good as anything he'd done. He took the time to
do them right. It would be a rare concert where a

lot of things were rehearsed.

He had something else planned for Miami. He had thought of something. Like Ken said, he knew that all along. Why didn't he think of it?

Cliff came in on a flight twenty minutes before Ken came in. Al greeted them. He'd come to the airport to meet them and explain what he was going to do. He wanted them there. He didn't know any Miami police.

They went to the hotel. Tomorrow was the concert. He introduced Johanna Kelvins, his new girlfriend. The whole band was there. He said he was going to marry Johanna and quit the business. If his wife was in danger of getting murdered if he was performing, he would stop performing. He would finish the contracts signed, but don't sign anymore.

George said he wished him the best. They were all millionaires. He had more money than he could spend for the rest of a luxurious life.

Arny said they could make millions more before they burned out. Why give it up?

"Arny has always been more interested in money than things of true value," George said. "We have to consider other things than money."

Arny said he guessed he was a bit greedy. He was raised with nothing and wanted security.

"But money isn't really security. The stock market keeps going down, and that devaluates the money. I'm buying gold and silver. They'll keep their value," Al pointed out. "Anyway, I might change my mind. I do love performing, most of the time. If I have a wife, I'll quit. It's not definite between Johanna and me. We do have small differences. We're both stubborn in certain things."

Arny perked up. He said Al was not really the type to stay serious with Johanna. She said things right there that wouldn't fit with what he always said he wanted.

Johanna pouted. Everyone knew Al wouldn't like that. Al gave her a look that said that. She tossed her head and walked out. That was another thing that Al wouldn't countenance.

"Well. I doubt you'll stay much interested in her," George said. "She seems a bit, er, self-centered."

"Yeah. I made a promise or two I wish I hadn't," Al agreed. "I'll work it out. Somehow.

"Well, about tomorrow night. I have a few numbers that should be popular. They're pretty dark. I suppose that's why I was seriously considering Johanna. She usually doesn't act like that."

"But she *does* act like that. Caution!" Arny said. "What about the songs?"

They discussed the songs a bit. Al sang a part of a couple. Everyone agreed that they were headed for the chart top already, and they'd never been performed.

They stayed at it until late, then broke it up. They'd rehearse the new ones in the morning. The rhythm and pattern were familiar enough to where they wouldn't have any problems with them.

Al spent the next day, most of it, around Miami with Cliff and wife and Ken. He was recognized everywhere. People would want their picture taken with him or his signature. When it got to be too much they would go to another section. Al was so used to it he didn't really much notice. Cliff and Ken were getting a charge out of being seen so much with such a celebrity. Cliff's wife, Roberta, liked the attention, at first, but you could see it was getting thin.

They went back to the hotel after a very good lunch in a little Cuban restaurant. Al liked the Cuban food, as did Cliff and Roberta. Ken hadn't tried it. He found it was very good, but a bit too picante for his taste.

Al went to the arena to check over the stage set-up and to practice a few tricky riffs for the new songs.

The time of the concert was approaching

Al Barker walked onto the stage, waved, sat on his famous stool, slung the guitar over his shoulder and welcomed everyone. Paul came to stand behind him to start a pattern on the bass.

Here comes the storm again.
Here come the wind and pain.
Here come the lonely nights.
Here come the silly fights.
Why do I stand this? This hurt and grief?
Why don't I tell you how I want relief?
'Cause you've got me in a vice.
You've made a mess of life,
Girl, there's the door.
I don't want to see you here no more.
I can only doubt you.
It's better for me without you.
Time to call it over.
Time that I got sober.
Time to say the truth.
Time I'm over you.

"That's tonight's pure crap song. Aren't you glad it's over?"

The audience hooted, laughed and applauded.

"I do like the first three lines. It goes down the slide from there."

He tuned the "E" string on his guitar. "I didn't change the whole set. This one will wander. You'd think, after all the years I've played, I'd know that.

"Oh, well. If you're wondering what the hell's going on, I'm trying to think of a song, but nothing new seems to be there. As Archie Bunker said to the psychiatrist, 'You don't need to check out my head. There's nothing in there.'

"I know. Half of you have no idea who Archie Bunker was. Is. Whatever."

He had the string tuned. He hit an A minor.

Don't think about me when I'm gone, Irene.
Don't let me cross you mind.
We can't seem to bring it together now.
God knows how hard we've tried.
We find in little ways the way to make a better day,
Then we fall into some stupid phase
And chase the dream away.
Over and over have we made this cross we bear.
Over and over we can't find a thing to share.
Let's say goodnight and hope tomorrow brings
Us something that will make the things
We need come to us one more time.

He stopped. "And I said no more crap. It seems I lied. Sorry. I'm in a lousy mood. Life sucks, sometimes."

"Hey, Al!" Paul yelled. "Cloudy Days?"

He nodded. Might as well.

When we come together on the streets or in a

place,
We have to try to show another face.
One of bright smiles and pretended sweet surprise.
Deep down the both of us can't help but know
That this charade will bring a pain that only grows
Until the time they say it right out loud,
"You two have got your heads up in the clouds."
Cloudy days can make me feel the hurt inside
Can make me see that there are things,
Things that, try as we might, we can never hide.
I'll always care about you.
I'll always see the pain that grew
From seeds that we saw planted
On a cloudy day.

The words didn't say much, but the music made it a popular hit. It had a lot of intricate blues guitar and keyboard lead. It was a thing made by the music, not the lyrics. Al's songs always featured the whole band.

Al was doing this for a reason. Cliff came in at the left entrance and nodded. It had worked, to one extent or another. Now to see what developed.

Wait for me around the corner.
We can't be seen together here.
Walk by me like a total stranger.

Wait for me around the corner.
If someone comes along, just walk on by.
Another time we'll live within the lie.
You married him when we broke up
The hundredth time.
I married her to show whose heart was stronger.
What fools we mortals be.
Now we both cry ourselves to sleep at night.
We live alone within a self-made plight.
Wait for me around the corner.
We'll say "goodbye" the thousandth time.
But we both know when next we pass,
We've earned the pain that evermore will last.
Wait for me around the corner.
No one will see us crying for the time
We could meet, embrace and smile.
It's false. It's not there anymore.
Pretend that you're just going to the store.
We'll say "goodbye" again, but we both know
Tomorrow, a different corner, a different street
Where we can hide from others when we meet.
Wait for me around the corner.
And leave your pride there on the other side.

Pure country from the fifties. There was a big audience who liked that. A lot of the Latins in Miami related to the old style music. The crowd liked that one.

Time for rock.

It's getting later every day.
I only called you up for me to say
It's over when you make me sit and sigh.
Girl, get your ass away from my front door.
I can't waste time in trying anymore.
Go on home to Mama. Tell about me to your
Papa.
Just don't forget who started this sexy thing.
You think you own me.
Get over it. You don't.
You think you'll hurt me, but you won't.
Remember two can play this little game.
I might just be a little hard to tame.
'S been fun. Got to run. Got mine. Feelin' fine.

He hit the hard rhythm on chorus. Billy brought up the level of the wall of sound effects. Paul did a rolling bass

This was a growling, high sound number. He hit the gravelly voice right on cue. This one would have them dancing in the aisles. It was another one where the music made the song.

Hey girl it's almost supper time.
The afternoon's been much more than fine.
Go home to Mama. Tell her a few more lies.
"Hey Mom! I spent the afternoon
"At Martha's Fancy Hair Saloon."
She'll get that tight look on her face.
She can never tell you time and place

She had her own little sexy thing.
She was a player, just like you and me.
It's life. We live it more or less the same
And never tell our kids about our shame.
You and me, too, in later life
When our own kids will cause the strife.
'S been fun. Got to run. Got mine. Feelin' fine.

Lots of catcalls and hoots. They loved it. The sexier girls were in the aisle, shaking it.

The rest of the show was better and better. It started slow, but ended 'way up there.

Would they do another show before this was over?

Or did things happen like he hoped they would.

He went backstage to find Cliff, Roberta, Ken, Arny and George already there. Cliff smirked.

"Great show!" George cried. "It started like it would bust, but you pulled it out and over!"

"We can't just give this up!" Arny wailed.

"Oh, I'm half-decided to go awhile longer. It's a matter of getting the spine to get some things out of my life. I went after the wrong thing at the wrong time.

"Where is Johanna?"

"She went to the hotel," Cliff answered. "She said she had a headache and you weren't going to be in a good mood because you were blowing this gig big-time."

"She got a call on her cell," Roberta said. "She said it was her sister, that she had to see someone."

"She doesn't have a sister," Al replied, looking suspicious and a little mad. He noted a smug, satisfied look.

They talked a bit. Al said he was tired. He was going to sack out. Ken said he would go back to the hotel, himself. He was tired. Al could walk fifty miles in Miami's heat and not notice it. He couldn't.

They got a cab.

"How did you work it?" Al asked.

"Waited 'til she left. One of us managed to be with both of them all the time. He couldn't get away.

"When will he try again?"

"As soon as he can. Here in Miami. We'll be going to places where we know a lot of people for awhile day after tomorrow."

"How close do we play it?"

"Close. I think she can take care of herself."

They went to their rooms and turned in. Johanna said it went down pretty much the way he thought it would.

"Which one?"

"Don't know. Slightly disguised voice. It could have been either one. Or someone else."

He nodded. They went to bed. She was there, he was a normal sort. No promises, no lies. It was for fun.

Two days. They would have proof within two days. He would have trouble controlling himself for that two days.

Al spent the next morning editing the CD. It was a matter of course that each show had its CD. They didn't do studio recordings anymore. Experience showed them that the live performances produced a lot more hits than the studio ones.

Cliff and Ken would stay the extra day or two as guests of the band. They wanted to be in on the ending of the murder case. Al wanted to see if it was from orders from somewhere else of a personal thing.

Everything was going particularly well, so far as the music business went. They had another hit CD coming out. Al didn't care one way or another if he got a million or two from it. He didn't know what to do with what he had. He gave a lot to children's funds and to AIDS research and such. The whole band did.

Arny and George came in George wanted to know if he had made anymore of a decision about leaving the business. He said it was a matter of getting some things in life squared away. They could see from the show last night that he couldn't concentrate when he had things like that hanging over his head. He couldn't continue without someone in his life. Johanna wasn't that someone, but he wasn't about to put anyone he really cared for in that position. He had let her get a little too much into his head. She was really a good person, if a bit spoiled. ... he was confused. At times he was turned off by her, at others, turned on.

He let her get in the way of his music. That was a worry with him. He wasn't sure he could do much of the kinds of things that sold with her between him and creativity.

He went to the hotel later. He would take Ken and Roberta and Cliff on a tour toward the south, around Homestead. They would be back about five. Johanna would go with them. Ken asked about that.

"Narrow the time frame. It will have to be tonight."

"But, well, how much does she know?" Ken asked.

"All of it! I didn't tell you that?"

"No. I thought you wouldn't use anyone for bait in something like that, but I also thought you had made if safe, even if she didn't know much," Cliff said.

"She's been a close friend for years. Part of it

was her idea when I told her about my suspicions. Everyone who could be the killer was accounted for, then I remembered that Arny and George could disappear for an hour or more and no one could be sure. They managed to be seen at times in the crowd. If they weren't there for a part of the show, we wouldn't know it.

"I never considered them. It was the guys who said they knew damned well where each of us were every minute. We only knew where they were when we happened to see them in the crowd. Fifty thousand people. They could be lost, but right there all the time. They could also be gone and we wouldn't know it.

"I first wondered if it was both of them. Maybe under orders of their bosses. I think we would have them both, if it was that. I still don't know if it was from orders."

Cliff nodded. "I had that suspicion from the first, but knew there was no way I could prove it."

Ken said, "If Greco would have thought of that, think what would happen!"

"That horse's ass!" Cliff spat. "He would march around, arrest them both, and try to intimidate them to give each other up. They would confuse and cover and we would never know."

"We'll know. Tonight or tomorrow."

"There's a little thing or two they don't know

about me," Johanna, who had just come in, said. She and Al giggled a bit. They said it would be a surprise to them.

"Not to me," Cliff said, grinning. "I checked on you as soon as your name came up. You hold a third degree black belt in Kohishi tae-kwan-do."

She bowed and grinned. "I know all forty two ways to kill using only your hands, feet and head. I know more ways to make you wish to whatever gods you believe in that I'd allow you to die.

"I'll call you in as soon as I've been attacked – or maybe an hour or two later."

Roberta giggled. "She showed me a little thing or two. Get out of line with me and you'll regret it!"

"Honey! I didn't mean *that*!" Cliff cried. They all laughed.

It was a lot lighter. They went to Homestead, stopping at several places on the way. They had a very good day. They made plans. Johanna had a little locator bug she would wear in a brooch. It also had audio.

They got back and went to the hotel. Johanna managed to be seen going into the bookshop off the lobby after dinner. Cliff, Ken and Al were going to be in the studio. They said they wanted to know a bit more about that end of the business.

They were at the studio. The band had gone

home.

At just before nine the signal came on that Johanna had been contacted. They turned on the recorder and speaker. They also had an intercept on her cell phone number.

"Hello. It's your quarter."

"This is the friend of Allen who called you at the concert. I was detained and unable to make the appointment, for which I humbly apologize.

"Can you meet me tonight? Now?"

"Well, I guess ... Al's not here. I'm just getting something to read. I don't think ... well, if it's close."

"Very well. Do you know where the Horseshoe Crab Bar is?"

"No."

"Any cab will know. Just say, 'The Horseshoe Crab.' It's only a few minutes away. Walking distance, but you don't want to walk around the streets alone at night. I don't want to take the chance you might be assaulted or mugged or anything."

"Well, okay, I guess. I'll put the books in the room and put on something and ... half an hour?"

"Don't dress up. It's a little local bar. Come as you are."

"Oh, okay. Fifteen minutes. I want to put on lipstick and that."

"Fine. I'll be there."

"Know it?" Al asked.

Cliff checked his Blackberry. "About three blocks from here. On that little creek. It's closed Sundays."

Al grabbed a camera. "Let's get there first. We can find a way to where they'll be that we can use to take a little video of our own."

They went out and to the little palm frond bar. There was no one about. They came in from the back side and around to the area behind a bamboo reed wall. Al quickly set up the camera. It was special for low light. There was a small light left on in the room all the time. That camera was wide-angle enough to get the whole room from where he had it hidden. He had a black tape across the red "On" light.

Six minutes later Arny came to look over the room. He smirked and put a ski mask over his head and went to stand in the shadows by the door to the room.

A taxi came, dropped Johanna off, and left. She stood, looking uncertain as she looked up and down the road.

"Miss Kelvins?" Arny called.

"Yes? Where are you?"

"Here by the bar." He stepped out to where she could see him, if not very clearly. "We can use the table room. I am friends of the owner. He knows I'm here. I have his permission and the keys."

She came slowly over. He stepped inside before she could see he had on the ski mask.

She came in. He grabbed her and tried to get her around the throat.

He screamed a high-pitched scream. He was suddenly in intense pain. She stepped in front of him and brought up her knee. Hard. He was on the ground, sobbing and retching.

"You ain't gonna ever be a father, Sucker!" she said. "What a crud! It usually takes me three or four seconds to ruin a crud. You? Two seconds! What a crud!"

He squeaked.

"You on your own, or you got a sponsor!"

He sobbed, then tried to scream, but nothing came out. "I asked you a question!"

"Muh – muh – me."

"Why, Crud?"

"The money! Oh, God! Please! No more! Please!"

"What money? You got a few million now, Crud!"

"The concert. It made four million. Oh, God!"

"So? Why the next one?"

He shook his head and tried to sit up. He

suddenly started a scream that cut off abruptly.

"You don't learn so easy, do you? I asked a question."

"I thought he'd do another concert!"

"He did."

"It wasn't what I wanted. I wanted another tribute. He writes fantastic stuff that makes millions when he's ... oh, God!"

"Gonna make another few million by knocking me off, Crud?"

"No! You were because ... yes! Okay! Yes!

"Gheeeee!"

"He's all yours, Al. What's left of him."

Al turned off the camera. He was going to do a little thing or two on his own.

He took a look at Arny, laying there, groaning and sobbing.

He wasn't worth it.

"We've got a confession. Let's tie it up," Ken suggested. They all agreed.

<u>Dark Corners</u>

We live our lives in fear of turning a dark corner.

The dark is coming only from those fears.
We know a little trepidation,
That going there will bring us nought but tears.
We find ourselves in crazy situations.
We try to face the truth about the facts of life.
About the pain and suffering and strife.
So many times we bring those things to light
From ignorance, not knowing which is right.
Dark corners, let me face mine.
Let me know where life will lead.
A road to a place to match the sign.
Turn that corner when you reach it, not before.
Don't fret about what dark things lie in store.
Because most times they don't.

Strong reverb on guitars and keyboards as the break comes. Go up a key for the chorus. Lights up. Volume up. Presence up.

It's better that we seek our Bali Hai, to find that special place,
To live our lives at a smoother, slower pace –
But then, what happened to the excitement? To

the rush and thrill of danger?

We look in fear because we don't know the face of the terrible stranger

Who lurks below the surface in our minds.

Drop back to the lower key. Bring up the mid-tones to a lighter mood.

So face the fact that your deep dark corners

Are no more than fears that come from silly dreams.

Tell me and yourself about the many falsehoods

The things we fear that defy reality, the things that bring about an urge to scream

And let the face of that terrible stranger, up to no good

Fade away as we face a mirror of our troubled mind.

It's not true. It's not real. That is the truth you'll find.

Turn the corners when you reach them, not before.

Forget about the darker things you'll find there.

Because most times you won't.

It's better that we seek our Bali Hai, to find that special place,

To live our lives at a smoother, slower pace –

But then, what happened to the excitement? To the rush and thrill of danger?

We look in fear because we don't know the face

of the terrible stranger
Who lurks below the surface in our minds.
Stop the music, except the bass
That terrible stranger is a figment in your mind
... *mind* ... *mind* ...fading out on loop.

This was the first time they'd tried a Moody Blues type of thing. It worked. Moody's style of music was a thing that would always have appeal. It could reach a part of you.

The next was more Southern Rock, then an old bop kind of thing.

The concert was a success. The first of what would, hopefully, become a yearly gig was history. Al waved and left the stage to thundering applause. He'd written the last number right there, as was what people hoped to see. It wasn't his best, but it was far from his worst.

Tampa. Where all his worst nightmares started, then Miami, where they ended. Next year.

Al thought about it. They had pre-sold enough CDs to, with the gate and sidebars of this concert, make them a few million apiece.

Like any of them needed that.

Allen Barker would never leave music. That was because music would never leave Allen Barker.

Get over the hard spots and life could be good – if you let it.

C. D. Moulton's works are available on most major outlets as printed or e-books. CD writes the CD Grimes, PI, mysteries, the Det. Lt. Nick Storie mysteries, the Clint Faraday mysteries, the Flight of the Maita science fiction series, books on orchid culture and many others of many types. Mystery, adventure, intrigue, science fiction, humor, fantasy, paranormal, mild erotica, and factual.